Words to Know Before You Read

axle   Nixi

exit   Pax

extra   six

Extreme   toolbox

fix   wax

foxes   x-ray

www.rourkeeducationalmedia.com

Edited by Luana Mitten
Illustrated by Louise Anglicas
Art Direction and Page Layout by Tara Raymo
Cover Design by Renee Brady

Library of Congress PCN Data

Bus Troubles / Precious McKenzie
ISBN 978-1-62169-247-8 (hard cover) (alk. paper)
ISBN 978-1-62169-205-8 (soft cover)
Library of Congress Control Number: 2012952743

Rourke Educational Media
Printed in the United States of America,
North Mankato, Minnesota

rourkeeducationalmedia.com

customerservice@rourkeeducationalmedia.com • PO Box 643328 Vero Beach, Florida 32964

Bus Troubles

Bus Driver

Counselor Nixi

Counselor Quinn

Henry

Jack

Hana

Zoe

Rodney

Written By Precious McKenzie

Illustrated By Louise Anglicas

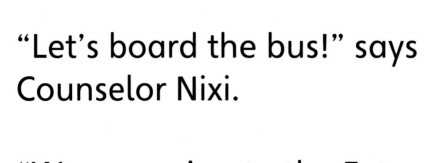

"Let's board the bus!" says Counselor Nixi.

"We are going to the Extreme Skate Park."

5

The bus bounces along the road.

"Uh-oh!" calls the bus driver.
"Hold on!"

6

treme
te Park

CAMP ADVENTURE

"Children, please exit the bus," says Counselor Quinn.

"Time to fix the problem," sighs the bus driver.

"What is wrong?" asks Counselor Nixi.

"Looks like a broken axle," says the bus driver.

"Oh no! We can't go!" sighs Rodney.

"Don't you have tools in your toolbox?" asks Zoe.

"I don't have an extra axle in my toolbox," says the bus driver.

"We will have to wait for a tow truck," says Hana.

"What can we do while we wait?" asks Henry.

13

"Let's sing a song," says Hana.

"I've got my xylophone," says Jack.

"Six little foxes went out to play, over the hills and far away," sing the children.

But soon they are bored.

"We can still use our skateboards. Let's wax that curb and skate while we wait," says Rodney.

"Time to grind," shouts Zoe.

"Uh-oh! Looks like I need an x-ray," cries Rodney.

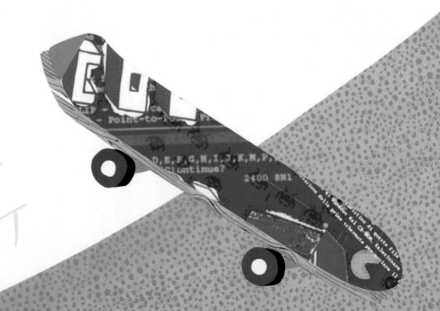

After Reading Word Study
Picture Glossary

Directions: Look at each picture and read the definition. Write a list of all of the words you know that have the *x* sound like *exit*. Can you find a word in this book that begins with an *x* but doesn't make the same sound as *x-ray*?

axle (AK-suhl): The axle is the rod that goes between the wheels of a vehicle. The wheels spin around the axle.

exit (EK-sit): When you exit something, you leave.

fix (FIKS): When something is broken, you fix it to put it back together.

foxes (FAHKS-ez): Foxes are wild animals that are in the dog family. Foxes have bushy tails and pointy ears.

six (SIKS): Six is the word for the numeral 6.

toolbox (TOOL-bahks): A toolbox is a box that is made to carry hand tools like hammers and wrenches.

wax (WAKS): When you wax something, you use a substance to make it smooth.

x-ray (EKS-ray): An x-ray is a picture of the inside of your body made by a special machine.

About the Author

Precious McKenzie lives with her family in Billings, Montana. She does not know how to fix broken axles or wax a curb to skateboard. Maybe she will learn how to do both someday!

Ask The Author!
www.rem4students.com

About the Illustrator

Louise Anglicas is a Manchester born illustrator now living in the Staffordshire Potteries with her partner and two young daughters. Her first job was as a ceramic designer which involved reading Harry Potter books, and then designing mugs and children's breakfast sets based on them! Louise loves to travel with her family. Her favorite thing to do on holiday is go to waterparks with very big slides!

Comprehension & Word Study:

- Retell the Story:

  Who are the main characters in the story?

  What happened to the bus?

  How did the students on the bus react to the problem?

  Have you ever had to entertain yourself or keep yourself occupied while an adult was busy doing something? What did you do?

- Word Study: A Silly Story With the Letter Xx

  Create a silly story using your sound words with the letter Xx. Include a main character, problem and solution, and setting. Share your story with a friend.

Sound Words I Used:

axle
exit
extra
extreme
fix
foxes
Nixi
Pax
six
toolbox
wax
x-ray

Let's Learn The **Xx** Sound

Bus Troubles

Sound Adventures

Sound Adventures is a fresh approach to traditional phonics based readers. With delightful stories, they build vocabulary and encourage readers to apply what they are learning about letters and sounds. Come along on wild journeys with the characters from Camp Adventure!

ISBN 978-1-6216-9205-8

90000

9 781621 692058

by

Rourke
Educational Media
rourkeeducationalmedia.com

A Blimp in the Blue

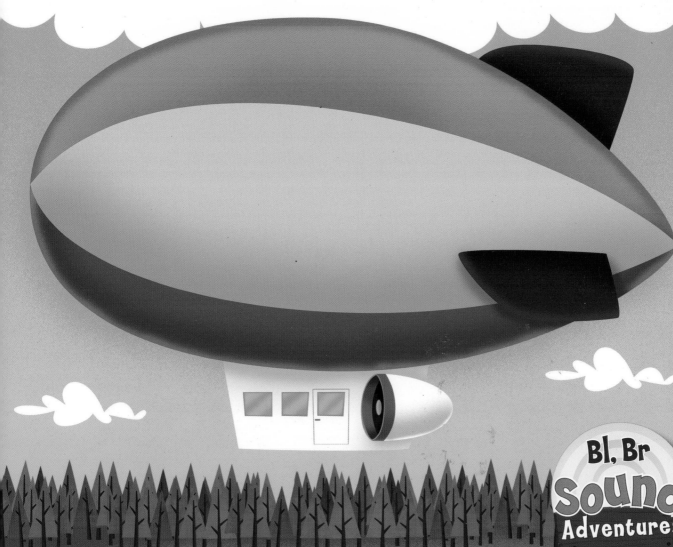

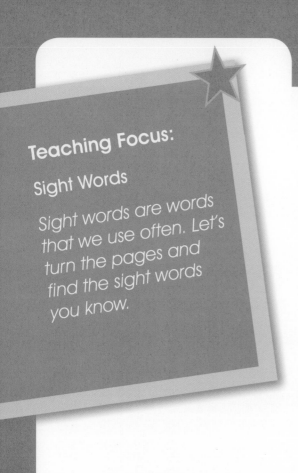

Teacher Notes available at
rem4teachers.com

Tips for Reading this Book with Children:

1. Read the title and make predictions about the story.

   Predictions – after reading the title have students make predictions about the book.

2. Take a picture walk.

   Talk about the pictures in the book. Implant the vocabulary as you take the picture walk.

   Have children find one or two words they know as they do a picture walk.

3. Have students look at the first pages of the book and find a word that begins with the letter or sound focus of the book.

4. Ask students to think of other words that begin with that same sound.

5. Strategy Talk – use to assist students while reading.
   - Get your mouth ready
   - Look at the picture
   - Think…does it make sense
   - Think…does it look right
   - Think…does it sound right
   - Chunk it – by looking for a part you know

6. Read it again.

7. Complete the activities at the end of the book.